The House of Hallucinations

Medhansh Pipaliya

CONTENTS

1 RON VISITS GRANDMA

A boy called Ron lived in a small village called Westsagton. He was known for his bravery and adventurous spirit. Every summer, he would visit his grandma's house. Even this summer, he saw his grandma. A decrepit old house, long abandoned, stood beside his grandma's house. Whenever Ron went to his grandma's house, he wondered about the mysteries hidden inside. However, his grandma always caught him whenever he attempted to sneak into that house because she was very alert. Whenever he tried to sneak in and someone caught him, he would always be furious at them and quarrel with them. Rumors of the house being haunted were why his grandma forbade him from sneaking inside. He tried to sneak in five or six times, consistently getting caught each time.

Ron's curiosity about the abandoned house only grew stronger with each failed attempt to explore it. He couldn't shake the feeling that there was something important hidden within its walls. Despite his anger at being caught, he couldn't resist the urge to try again. As the summer drew to a close, Ron knew he had to find a way to uncover the secrets of the mysterious house before it was too late.

A growing boredom with his repeated failed attempts at sneaking in led Ron to play cricket with his pals as his grandma kept an eye on them. The ball shattered a window in the haunted home after Ron struck a six, and then, out of nowhere, it was doubled; two balls dangled precariously from the shattered glass. Not even Ron's grandmother could believe it.

All of the people, including Ron himself, were taken aback when they saw the ball that had been reproduced. As they approached the glass with caution, they became aware that one of the balls appeared to be emitting a faint glow. When Ron stretched out and picked up the glowing ball, he felt a weird energy rushing through his veins. This peaked his curiosity, and he reached out for the ball. In his ignorance, he was unaware that this was merely the first of a string of mysterious occurrences that would take place over the course of the next few days.

By the time it was eight o'clock at night, Ron was already starving. Grandma had placed an order for dinner at a restaurant that is known all over the world. At the time when the food arrived, Ron was devouring enormous slices of pizza, and his grandmother was eating pizza that she had made herself. His grandma requested that he try a piece of pizza. It was disgusting to Ron, so he spit it out once he had a taste of it. Ron's grandma was angry, and he gazed at her with a disgusted expression on his face. His grandma was the one who was questioned, "What did you put in the pizza?" His grandmother said that she had included her enchanted and secret ingredient, which was only known to a select few.

Not a single person, not even Ron, was aware of what the peculiar component was. Because it was a closely guarded secret, only his grandmother's ancestors were aware of what it was. Ron persisted in his efforts to obtain the secret ingredient from his grandmother, but she remained reticent and insisted that it was a long-standing custom in the family to keep the component a secret. Ron, who was both frustrated and interested, made a solemn commitment to one day discover the truth about the miraculous chemical that his grandmother used.

In a short amount of time, they finished their meal and retired to bed. Despite the fact that Ron was sleeping, he awoke at midnight because he noticed that there was a light in the haunted house. After hearing his screams, his grandmother arrived as quickly as she could and inquired about what had transpired. Grandma, Ron told her that there was a light in the spooky house. Grandma's response was as follows: "If you are deceiving, I will batter you to a pulp!"

Then she looked out the window and saw a figure with blood-red eyes and pitch-black vision. As she took in the frightening scene, she became so terrified that she passed out. Ron went to get a bucket of water, and he started pouring it on his grandmother. As soon as she awoke, she asked, "WWhhho is innn the hhhaunteed hhoousse?" while shivering. Ron pleaded with Grandma, "I beg your pardon; don't you see that we are unable to see through the window? Do you want to go inside the house and make sure everything is in order? Oh,

I see." Grandma yelled out in a loud voice, "You dare speak to me like that, Ron!" His grandmother uttered the words, "You don't respect your grandma, Ron?" His grandmother yelled out, "You insolent little brat!"

Ron was fuming because he felt betrayed, and he scowled at his grandma. His face turned a deep shade of crimson, reflecting his intense anger. His grandma went out of the room. Ron felt guilty. He suffered from his harsh words and felt regret for them, tossing and turning all night in bed.. He replayed the conversation with his grandma in his mind, realizing the hurtful words he had used. He understood the importance of taking responsibility and resolving the conflict by offering a sincere apology. Ron resolved to approach his grandma the following morning, ready to express his deep regret for his disrespectful behavior and seek forgiveness.

It was morning, and he was dull. He didn't eat his breakfast or lunch. Finally, it was dinner time. He got up from his bed and went to the kitchen, and his grandma was also very dull. She had prepared cereal and milk. Yuck, what a pity! Ron didn't want to depress his grandma. He had already exceeded his limits the previous night; they both didn't speak. They ate quietly and went to sleep.

The next morning, Ron woke up early while his grandma was sleeping. He wrote "Sorry, Grandma" on a cake and left it on the table. His grandma woke up, surprised to see the cake on the table. After finding the cake, she went to Ron's bedroom to share breakfast with him. She knocked on the door and served breakfast to Ron. Ron saw pizza, his favorite food. He felt a mix of guilt and joy swirling in his stomach. He felt guilty and said sorry to his grandma. His grandma hugged him. He happily munched on the pizza. His stomach let out a loud, rumbling growl.

2 THE SKELETON

The next day, Ron sneaked into the house. He entered, and the door shut behind him. GRRR! He freaked out and called out that whoever was in the house would be a fool. Suddenly, a skeleton appeared in front of him. On the skull, there was a sentence. It said, "I'm not a nincompoop kid." The skull was stained with blood.

Ron tried to open the door and run out, but the door was locked from the outside. He wanted to faint, but he didn't want to give up. He saw a sword on the ground. He picked up the sword and decapitated the skeleton. This made the ghost even angrier.

At that moment, Ron felt pain in his stomach. Upon examining his stomach, he realized that the sword had stabbed him. He cried for help. His neighbors recognized Ron's panicked voice and quickly opened the door. They saw Ron lying unconscious on the floor. They took him to the hospital, and the doctor informed his family that he was in a coma that would last at least 5 years. Ron's distraught grandma started crying and immediately called his parents. They were horrified after hearing the news of Ron's coma and uncertain recovery.

3 A MIRACLE

Ron was in a coma, lying on a hospital bed. His heartbeat was decreasing slowly. The doctors told her that there was a very low chance he could survive. Then a miracle happened, and Ron started moving his fingers. This was a sign that he would most probably survive! After a few hours, he woke up, feeling no pain at all due to the anesthetics. He felt a sudden jolt of pain throughout his body due to the wound from the sword, and he passed out. The doctors operated on his wound and saw that metal had pierced his blood vessels. They then told his grandma that there was a 50-50 chance he would survive. His grandma and his parents decided to go for the surgery. After 7 hours of surgery, it was a success! His grandma was the happiest lady in the world. Ron was in the hospital for six more days, just in case.

He opened his eyes, and a yellow light was flashing on him. His grandma was talking to his parents on the phone. She handed the phone over to Ron. His parents were so worried about him. They sent Ron a get-well-soon gift full of medicines. He thought his parents were the weirdest and most worrisome parents on Earth! THUD! The door opened, and the doctor came marching in with a report. He looked at a big scar on Ron's stomach. It looked like a hammer, but with a large stick. He told them that the scar could not be erased. He was horrified, thinking that in school people would tease him and he would become the laughingstock over there. He asked the doctor if anything was to be done to remove the scar—literally anything. The doctor told him nothing was possible. He sulked on the bed. His grandma had given him a large gun that shot foam pellets. He thanked her and started playfully shooting every single nurse or doctor that came into the room. They ran away yelling; it was hilarious.

As he continued to play with the foam pellet gun, his mood began to lighten slightly. The nurses and doctors seemed to understand that he was just trying to cope with the news of his scar, and they even laughed along with him. Despite their initial shock, they were all kind and understanding towards him. Eventually, the boy's laughter turned into tears as he realized the gravity of the situation. He would have to face the world with this scar, and there was nothing he could do about it. But as he wiped away his tears, he remembered his grandmother's words of wisdom: "It's not about what's on the outside, but what's on the inside that truly matters." And with that thought in mind, he made a decision to embrace his scar and show the world that he was more than just his appearance.

4 THE POLICE

Ron was out of the hospital now, so he was free to go into the house again. His grandma watched him closely, making it impossible for him to leave. It was night, and his grandma went to sleep. He tiptoed out of the house and into the night. The stars were low in the sky, twinkling high above. The ground was still as dark as night, with the ghost lurking in the night. Ron pushed the door open; he was welcomed with a headbutt and knocked out. He was kidnapped. The ghost used magic to prevent him from getting away. The ghost gagged him and tied him to the ceiling. The ghost was resting because he overused his powers; he fell asleep. Ron tried to untie his hands, but he could not. He used his long and sharp nails to cut through the rope. He held on to the rope and slowly climbed down. He had escaped.

Suddenly, a dark force grabbed his neck and started strangling him. It strangled him to the point where he could not move. He lost consciousness as a result of the pain. His eyelids struggled to lift, but he saw a faint glimmer of light through the pale, blood-stained window. He could not move, but he was still conscious. He heard a faint sound of police sirens; his grandma had already called the police. The sirens got louder and louder until it felt like there were tens of police cars outside the house. He managed to open his eyes slightly and was welcomed with a stab in his left eye. He lifted his body as needle-sharp darts pierced through his left eye. He writhed on the ground, unable to contain his agony. An impulsive jolt of pain shot throughout his body.

Unable to move, he allowed a giant black anaconda to tighten its grip around his body. It squeezed Ron until every single one of his bones was broken. The house's wall shattered with a deafening roar. A police officer shot the anaconda three times in the head. Its grip loosened, and it lay there, not moving or making a sound. The ghost was trapped on the wall and sealed in a special container for ghosts. The police rushed Ron to the hospital; he was critical.

The doctor immediately took him to the operation theater, where he was under surgery. His grandma came to the hospital weeping while talking to Ron's parents. There was only a 10% chance of survival for Ron. His grandma was praying that her grandson would be fine. The light in the operation theater turned off, and a doctor came out. He told Ron's grandma there was bad news. She was devastated. Ron was no more; the ventilator had given up on him. His grandma did not believe it, so she went inside. Ron was lying on the bed, motionless. His grandma collapsed and called his parents. His mom could not handle it and passed out; she was in the hospital.

5 THE UNDERWORLD

Ron's funeral occurred, and he was buried in a graveyard. His family mourned him every day until the point where their eyes turned into a desert. A few months later, Grandma heard a knock on the door and opened it—she could not believe her eyes! Ron was there, standing in front of her. She hugged him, but her hands just passed through him; he was a ghost. Ron revealed to his grandma that the haunted house served as a gateway to the Underworld, the realm of Hades and Persephone. He also told her that the ghost that killed him was the guardian of the entrance, but since it was no longer there, she could go into the underworld and get him out of there.

He said goodbye and disappeared into the night. His grandma did not tell anybody and packed for her adventure. She packed all sorts of things—food, weapons, and maps. She went to the house and found a trapdoor on the floor. She lifted it and saw the underworld; it was dark and gloomy. It scared her to the core. She stepped in and saw billions of translucent people of all ages and types. They were divided into three sectors: the Elysium, the Asphodel Meadows, and the Fields of Punishment. Based on her knowledge, Ron would probably be in The Fields of Punishment for capturing the guardian of the entrance. It was a cracked wasteland with pools of lava; screams could be heard. A three-headed hellhound guarded the gate—the legendary Cerberus. It had a dragon for a tail and hundreds of heads of snakes on its back. Luckily, she had an invisibility cloak. She draped the invisibility cloak on herself and started walking towards the gate. She beat Cerberus! Now, she had to find Ron.

As she cautiously made her way through the Fields of Punishment, Ron's voice echoed in her mind. She remembered the last time they were together, laughing and joking as they explored the forests of their homeland. But now, everything has changed. The air was thick with despair, and the ground cracked beneath her feet. She knew she had to find Ron and bring him back to safety before it was too late. With determination in her heart, she pressed on, determined to rescue her friend from the clutches of the underworld.

6 FINDING RON

The Erinyes sisters (goddesses of vengeance) were torturing the prisoners in the most horrible ways possible. Hundreds of men, women, and children were being crucified; some were being boiled in lava; and some were being cooked inside brazen bulls for eternity. The scene filled her mind with horrifying images of her grandson enduring the same hideous torture methods. She carefully made her way through, making sure no one could spot her. She felt the ground shaking violently and sat down. There was a sizable golden chariot to her right, pulled by four pitch-black horses.

A massive figure with a shaggy beard and a solemn, mournful look occupied the chariot. He had a shaggy beard and a solemn, mournful look. It was Hades himself. His presence sent shivers down her spine. Hades was coming to the Fields of Punishment. Although she was sure she would be caught, to her relief, she was a sorceress with tricks up her sleeve. She used a spell to make herself one with the Underworld. Now, nobody could spot her. She had given Ron an enchanted necklace, imbued with protective spells to aid in times of peril.

She could teleport to Ron, wherever he was, but at a great cost—only once in a lifetime. She teleported and saw Ron; he was being crucified with a hundred dogs eating his body. His body was regenerating, and the dogs kept on eating. She slayed all the dogs and untied the ropes that held Ron. He fell with a thud. She lifted him up and started walking back to the entrance of the underworld. She pushed the trapdoor open and climbed back to the earth. They had both safely made it back.

Ron suddenly came back to life and hugged his grandma. Ron's grandma had saved him from a fate worse than death, and they both knew they would cherish this moment forever. The bond between them had grown even stronger through this harrowing experience.

7 CURSE OF THE UNDERWORLD

Grandma was talking to Ron's parents, but it was as if they were under an illusion. They never knew that Ron had died. Grandma hung up and started talking to Ron about his visit to the Underworld. He showed his grandma a mysterious symbol on his stomach that had appeared as soon as he returned from the underworld, hinting at a deeper connection to his journey. The symbol represented a curse, offering a glimmer of hope in the story. She knew it was ancient Greek, so she immediately decrypted it.

Whispered was the name Hades, the Lord of the Dead, in tones so solemn and deep. He, with promises to keep,
is tortured by nightmares; he never finds sleep.
In the darkness of his mind, he is forever kept.
Sleep eludes him, like a fleeting dream, a prisoner of his thoughts, a relentless stream.
Revenge, a promise, a man shall keep. A

solemn vow, in shadows deep. With a burning heart and eyes that gleam, he walks the path of a vengeful dream.

In the depths of the underworld, where shadows reign, A realm of darkness, a haunting domain. Where whispers echo and secrets lie, A place where lost souls forever cry.

In vain did Hades, Lord of the Dead, reign.

A realm of darkness and despair, where sorrow dwells.

Where do the spirits of the dead forever go?

In my realm, no mortal shall dare tread where power and darkness intertwine and are widespread. As a sovereign ruler, I stand tall and strong. My reign is unyielding, where mortals don't belong.

Soon, in pain they shall perish.

His grandma sent him home. He took one last look at her and the you-know-what house and left in a cab. As he drove away in the cab, the lingering unease from his grandmother's cryptic warning stayed with him, impossible to shake off. The ominous words echoed in his mind, intensifying his sense of foreboding about what awaited him upon his return home. A deep voice echoed in his mind: "You were fortunate to escape unscathed; I am unable to curse you due to ancient laws. Remember, should you trespass into my domain again, I will ensure your disintegration." Suddenly, the mark on his stomach disappeared, relieving him.

9 798894 758466